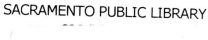
Sweet Pea & Friends
Alpaca Lunch

By John and Jennifer Churchman

L B

LITTLE, BROWN AND COMPANY
NEW YORK   BOSTON

Young Poppy the alpaca stood outside the barn with her mother, admiring the beautiful spring flowers. "What would you like to do today?" her mother asked.

"I want to go exploring!" Poppy replied.

"I thought you might," said her mother. "Perhaps you'll find some new foods for your lunch. All the spring fruits and vegetables are ready for you to try."

There was nothing Poppy liked more than discovering new things around the farm. "Okay, I'll try," she said.

Poppy walked through the meadow, where she saw Maisie the sheepdog watching one of her puppies taste a flower. "I'm finding new foods to try," Poppy said proudly.

"There are plenty of spring dandelions," said Maisie with a smile.

Dandelions? For lunch? Poppy hesitated, then took a nibble. They tasted so fresh and spicy!

The next day, Poppy brought her friends Lindsey and Brooks to the maple forest to see what foods they could find.

They saw the lambs Lilly and Petal in the shade under the trees. "What are you eating?" asked Poppy.

"Fiddlehead ferns," said Lilly. "They're my favorite spring treat."

"Mine, too," said Petal.

So Poppy and her friends foraged for ferns, ramps, trout lilies, and trillium flowers, and they all had a forest feast for lunch.

As spring turned to summer, Poppy explored the farm with her friends, finding more and more new foods for lunch. One day she brought her big sister Ria to the pond, where they found Keeper the goose with her baby goslings. "What are you eating?" asked Poppy.

"BUGS!" peeped the littlest gosling.

"And yellow marsh marigold flowers, purple violets, red clover, and fresh green mint," added Keeper.

Ria looked at Poppy. "Do we have to try *everything*?" she whispered.

"Maybe just the flowers and mint," Poppy said with a laugh. They left the bugs alone!

Early one summer morning, Poppy watched Farmer Jennifer and her daughter Gabby weeding and watering the kitchen garden. After they left, Poppy walked among the plants and saw Bella the cat hiding in the catnip. "I'm finding things for my lunch," said Poppy politely.

"I can share my catnip," said Bella, her bright-green eyes shining.

"Thank you!" said Poppy. "Would you try some new things with me, too?"

Bella nodded, and together they tasted green snow peas, garlicky scapes, chives, basil, parsley, and dill, and nibbled on fresh red strawberries for dessert.

Poppy was getting so good at finding new foods that she and her best friend, Lindsey, decided to explore the greenhouse. Together they peered in and saw the sheepdog puppies trying to nap. They also saw tomatoes of every color and cucumbers hanging on prickly vines. It looked like Farmer John had just finished picking some colorful peppers.

"I think we've found our lunch," Lindsey said with a giggle, accidentally waking up the puppies, who scampered outside.

Following the puppies, the friends nudged open the garden gate. They saw Laddie the sheepdog playing with the puppies as they tumbled from Farmer John's garden cart and climbed back up again.

Laddie suggested that Poppy and Lindsey try one of each of the colorful summer vegetables: lettuces and chard, spinach and broccoli, kale, carrots, red-striped beets, and summer squash in green and yellow. So they did!

On a late-summer day, Poppy called her alpaca friends together for lunch. "Let's go to the berry patch and see if they're finally ripe," she told them excitedly.

Following Poppy, the friends peeked through thorny brambles, where blackberries, raspberries, and elderberries hung heavy on the branches. They played in the sun and ate juicy berries all afternoon.

Summer was now turning into autumn, and a sweet smell was in the air. Poppy followed her nose all the way to the fruit orchard. "Hello, Poppy. What brings you here?" asked Sadie the pony.

"I smelled something wonderful," Poppy said.

"It's the fruit trees, grapes, and honey from the beehives," Sadie said, showing Poppy rosy-red apples, golden-yellow pears, sweet cherries, and dark-purple plums hanging on the orchard trees.

As Poppy and Sadie ate, they watched butterflies and listened as the sound of buzzing honeybees filled the air. "I think autumn might be my favorite time of year," said Poppy.

But a few weeks later, as Poppy walked to Farmer John's garden with her friends, she noticed frost on the flowers and grass. *That's never been there before*, she thought to herself.

Then she saw that the cornstalks had been cut and gathered into a shock, and the pumpkins and squash were in piles around the garden. *This doesn't look right,* Poppy thought. She was worried.

That night, Poppy stood outside the barn in the chilly evening air with her mother and the other alpacas. A yellow moon was rising. "That is the harvest moon," said her mother. "See the Canada geese flying south? They know winter is coming. Soon, everything on the farm will rest until spring."

Everything? Poppy wondered about her favorite gardens, the pond, and the forest. Would they rest, too?

When Poppy woke up the next morning, she looked out the frosty barn window and saw a blanket of snow covering the gardens!

The pond was frozen, and the forest trees were losing their leaves! "What will we eat now?" she asked her mother.

"I'm very proud of you for trying so many foods this year, Poppy," said her mother. "What were some of your favorite things to eat around the farm?"

Poppy thought about the spring, summer, and autumn. Everything she had tried was so good! "The lilacs in the spring, the kale in the summer, and the apples in the autumn," she decided.

"Come with me," her mother said, beckoning to Poppy and her friends.

Poppy's mother pushed open the door at the far end of the barn. Poppy couldn't believe her eyes!

There were pumpkins and apples, corn, squash, and hay. There were sweet red beets, cabbages, and kale—her favorite! Every color of the garden was heaped into big piles and baskets.

"Farmer John and Farmer Jennifer have stored food from the gardens for us," said her mother. "We will have plenty to eat all winter."

"Hurray!" said Poppy.

"Hurray!" cheered her friends.

That evening, as her mother kissed her good night, Poppy dreamed about what she would eat for lunch tomorrow, and what new things she would find next year.

Poorhouse Farm has many places that grow food for the farm family and for the animals, such as the forest, the pond, the greenhouse, and the kitchen garden. Poppy also wanders into the fruit orchard, the berry patch, and, of course, Farmer John's vegetable garden! How many of the foods on these pages have you seen before? How many of them have you tried?

In the **spring**, look for fiddlehead ferns, lettuce, peas, and spinach.

In the **summer**, look for tomatoes, beets, kale, and broccoli.

In the **fall**, look for corn, peppers, and carrots.

In the **winter**, look for pumpkins, squash, and apples (in storage!).

Sweet Pea says,
"Eat your greens!"

The True Story of Poppy

Poppy is a young Huacaya (pronounced *wuh-kai-ya*) alpaca who lives on Moonrise Farm with her mother and eleven other alpaca friends. She is very independent and curious, and she loves to explore the farm fields, forests, and gardens, looking for new things to eat.

Alpacas are social and affectionate animals, and they talk to one another (and to us!) by making humming, hawing, and orgling noises. Their coats are made of a soft and luxurious fiber that is turned into yarn once a year after the alpacas are sheared (given haircuts) each spring. They are also gentle on the land and ecosystem; their padded hooves and soft way of walking don't damage the undergrowth or the field grasses.

Poppy is intelligent and charming, with her tufted ears, long neck, and big, sweet eyes. She is a favorite with her farmyard friends and with us!

Special Thanks

This book was created with the support and encouragement of friends, family, and followers of Poppy and Moonrise Farm online. We would like to thank our agent, Brenda Bowen; editors, Megan Tingley and Deirdre Jones; and the whole team at Little, Brown Books for Young Readers. We'd also like to give a special thanks to all the booksellers in the Vermont area and beyond who have championed our books.

The story doesn't end here! Join the animals for more adventures at sweetpeafriends.com.

Dedicated with love to our children, Kailie, Travis, and Gabrielle;
to our nieces, Elizabeth, Sara, and Cailin, for thinking of every type
of fruit and vegetable; and to John's brother, Chad,
who loved working in the garden.

Little, Brown and Company
Hachette Book Group
1290 Avenue of the Americas, New York, NY 10104
Visit us at LBYR.com

First Edition: July 2018

Little, Brown and Company is a division of Hachette Book Group, Inc.
The Little, Brown name and logo are trademarks of Hachette Book Group, Inc.

The publisher is not responsible for websites (or their content) that are not owned by the publisher.

Library of Congress Cataloging-in-Publication Data
Names: Churchman, John, 1957– author, illustrator. | Churchman, Jennifer, author.
Title: Alpaca lunch / by John and Jennifer Churchman.
Description: First edition. | New York : Little, Brown and Company, 2018. | Series: Sweet Pea & friends |
Summary: Poppy the alpaca explores Moonrise Farm with her animal friends, finding and trying new foods
throughout the spring, summer, fall, and winter.
Identifiers: LCCN 2017043581| ISBN 9780316411608 (hardcover) | ISBN 9780316411639 (ebook) | ISBN
9780316411646 (library edition ebook)
Subjects: | CYAC: Farm life—Fiction. | Alpaca—Fiction. | Domestic animals—Fiction. |
Animals—Food—Fiction. | Food—Fiction. | Seasons—Fiction.
Classification: LCC PZ7.1.C55 Al 2018 | DDC [Fic]—dc23
LC record available at https://lccn.loc.gov/2017043581

ISBNs: 978-0-316-41160-8 (hardcover)
978-0-316-41161-5 (ebook)
978-0-316-41165-3 (ebook)
978-0-316-41163-9 (ebook)

Printed in China

1010

10 9 8 7 6 5 4 3 2 1